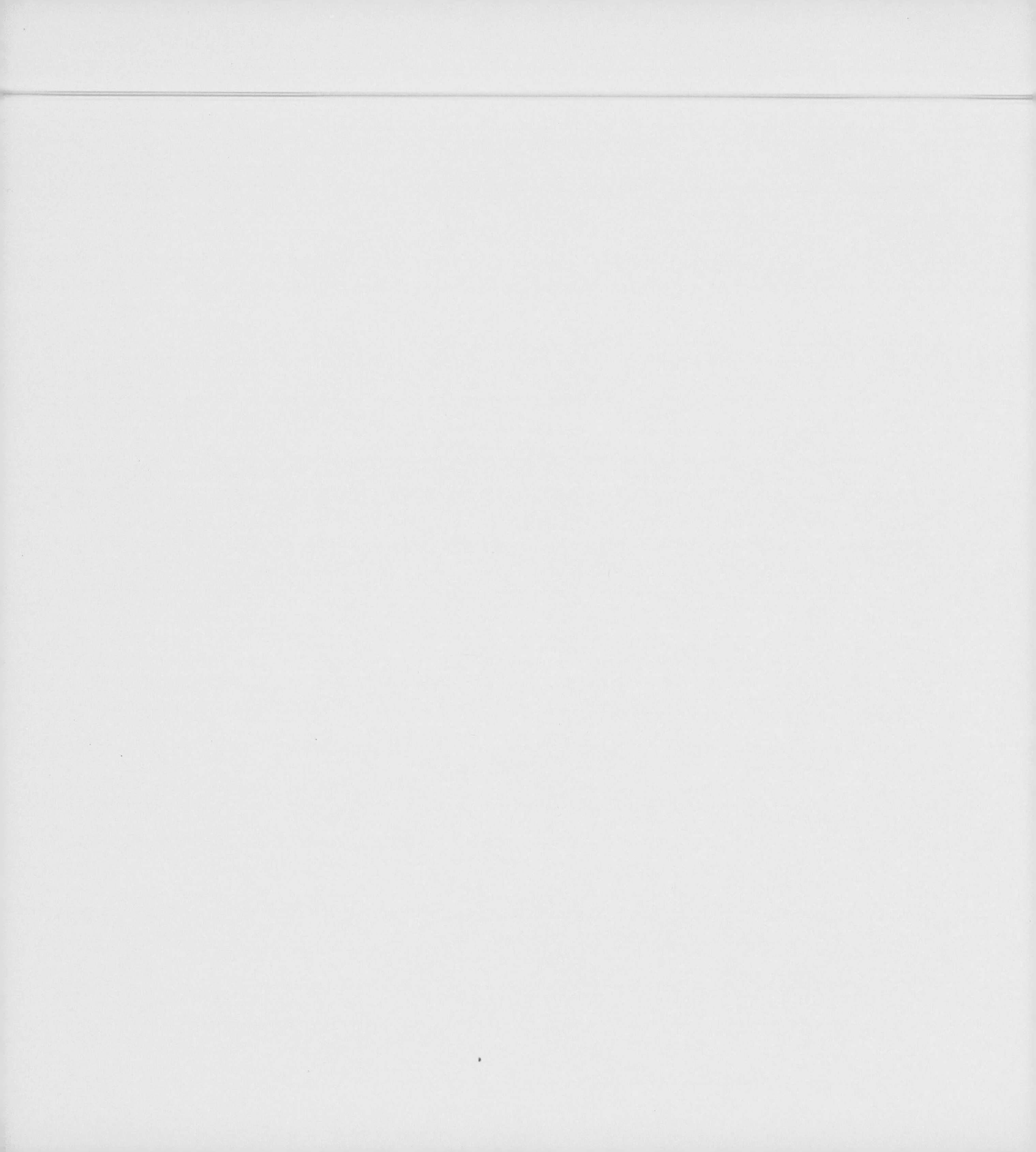

Bonnie & Ben Rhyme Again

Mem Fox
and
Judy Horacek

Beach Lane Books
New York London Toronto Sydney New Delhi

For Sarah Hatton—M. F.

For Ben and Jack—J. H.

BEACH LANE BOOKS
An imprint of Simon & Schuster Children's Publishing Division
1230 Avenue of the Americas, New York, New York 10020

Originally published in Australia in 2018 by
Scholastic Australia Pty Limited
This edition published under license from Scholastic Australia Pty Limited
First US edition, 2020

The text for this book was set in Lomba.
The illustrations for this book were rendered in ink and watercolor.
Manufactured in China
1119 SCP
10 9 8 7 6 5 4 3 2 1
Library of Congress Cataloging-in-Publication Data
Names: Fox, Mem, 1946– author. | Horacek, Judy, illustrator.
Title: Bonnie and Ben rhyme again / Mem Fox ; illustrated by Judy Horacek.
Description: First edition. | New York : Beach Lane Books, [2019]
Summary: Siblings Bonnie and Ben impress Skinny Doug with
their ability to recite nursery rhymes.
Identifiers: LCCN 2019010470 | ISBN 9781534453524 (hardcover : alk. paper)
Subjects: | CYAC: Stories in rhyme. | Nursery rhymes—Fiction.
Classification: LCC PZ8.3.F8245 Bm 2019 | DDC [E]—dc23
LC record available at https://lccn.loc.gov/2019010470

Bonnie and Ben were a boisterous pair
who loved yelling rhymes in the open air,
so they said their goodbyes
with a kiss and a hug,
and went out for a walk
with their friend Skinny Doug.

Skinny Doug was the one who, time after time,
had kept them entranced with rhyme after rhyme.
So, as they set off, he said,

"Where will you start?
You now know so many—
you know them by heart!"

Soon a small hill appeared up ahead.
There was no hesitation!

The two of them said:

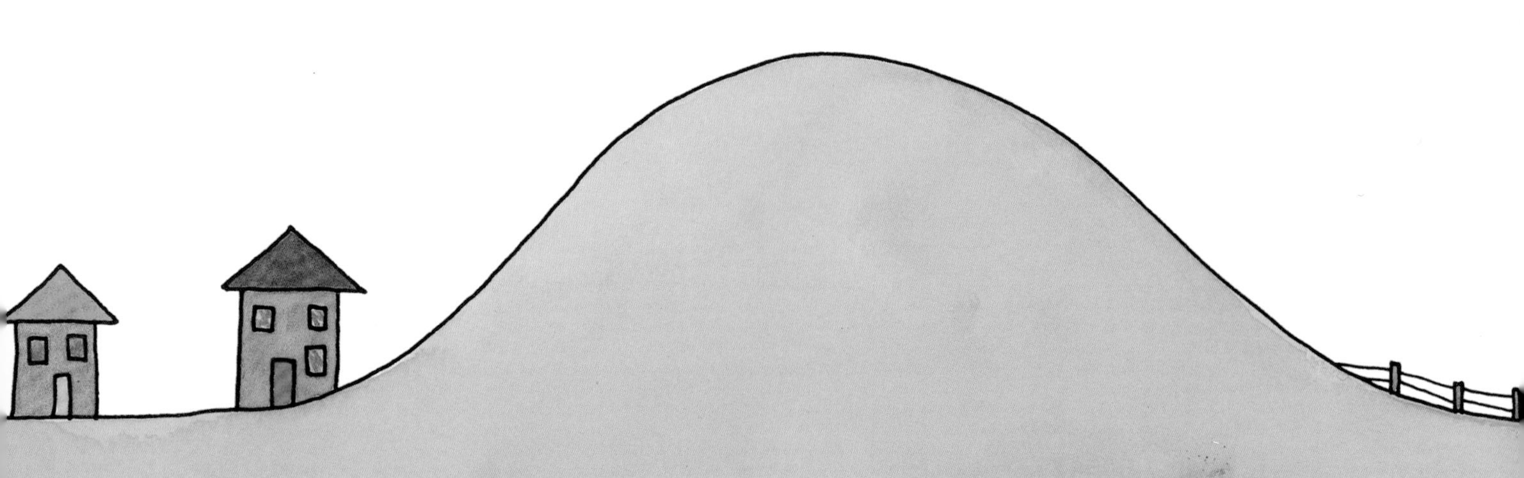

"Jack and Jill went up the hill,
to fetch a pail of water.

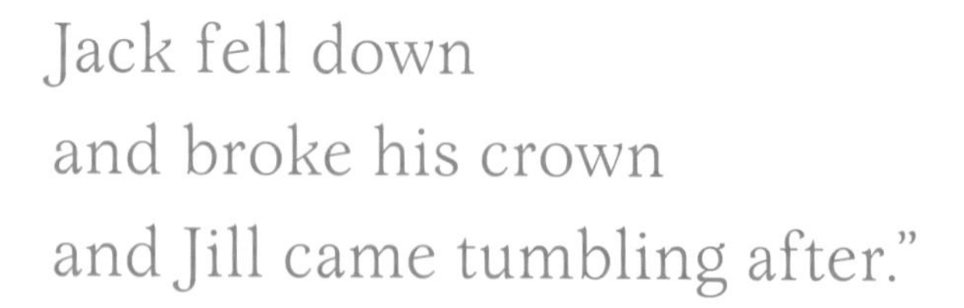

Jack fell down
and broke his crown
and Jill came tumbling after."

And Skinny Doug said:
"I love it, I love it!
Well done, and hurrah!

Can you tell me another?
How clever you are!"

When a couple of sheep appeared up ahead,
there was no hesitation!

The two of them said:

"Little Bo Peep has lost her sheep
and doesn't know where to find them.

Leave them alone
and they'll come home,
bringing their tails
behind them."

And Skinny Doug said:
"I love it, I love it!
Well done, and hurrah!

Can you tell me another?
How clever you are!"

When plums on a plum tree appeared up ahead,
there was no hesitation!

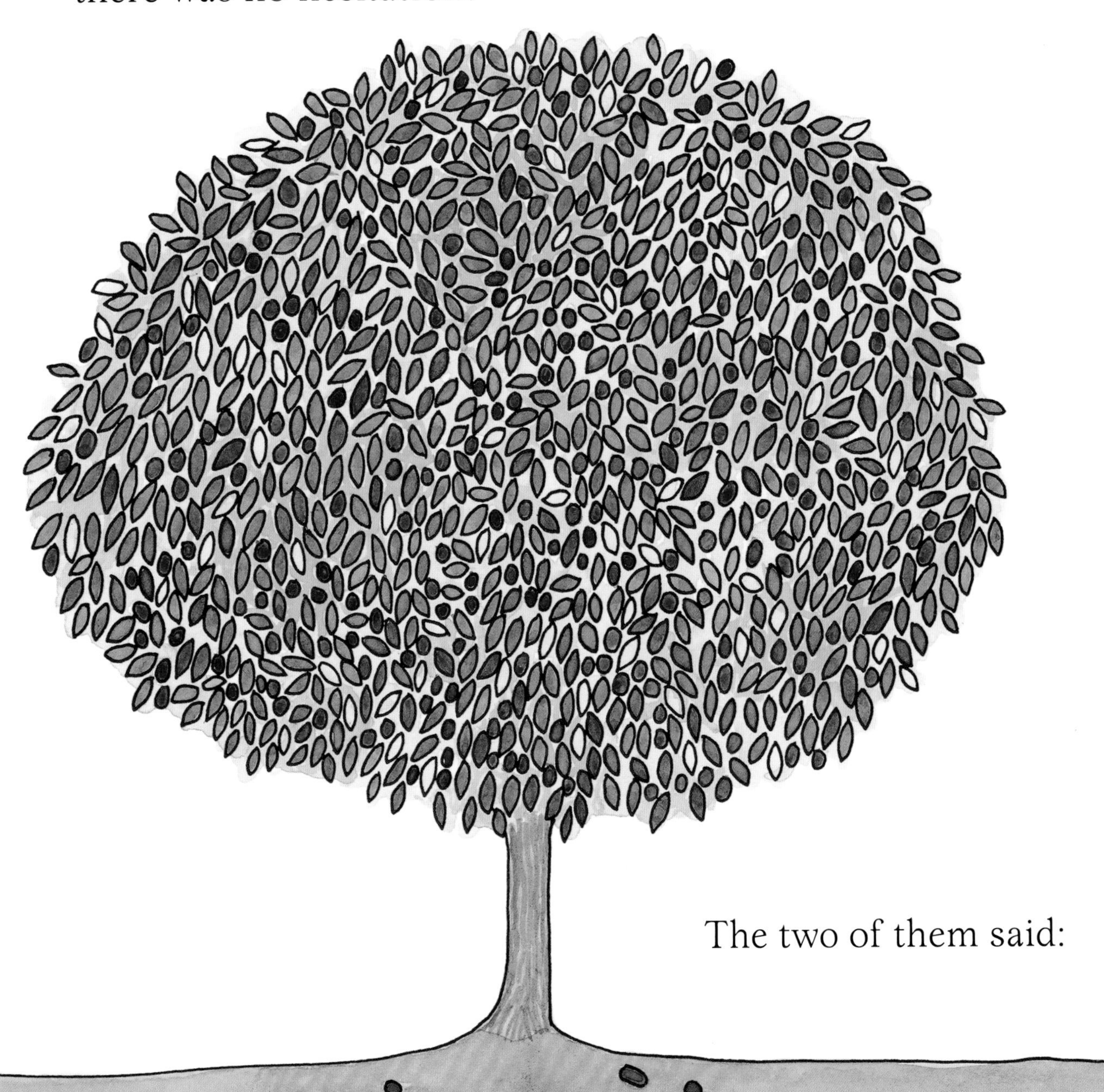

The two of them said:

“Little Jack Horner
sat in a corner,
eating his pudding and pie.

He stuck in his thumb
and pulled out a plum
and said, ‘What a good boy am I!’”

And Skinny Doug said:
"I love it, I love it!
Well done, and hurrah!

Can you tell me another?
How clever you are!"

When a hairy black spider appeared up ahead,

there was no hesitation!
The two of them said:

"Little Miss Muffet
sat on her tuffet,
eating her curds and whey.

Along came a spider,
who sat down beside her
and frightened Miss Muffet away."

And Skinny Doug said:
"I love it, I love it!
Well done, and hurrah!

Can you tell me another?
How clever you are!"

When magnificent roses appeared up ahead,
there was no hesitation!

The two of them said:

"Ring around the rosie,

a pocket full of posies!

Ashes, ashes,
we all fall down!"

And Skinny Doug said:
"I love it, I love it!
Well done, and hurrah!

Can you tell me another?
How clever you are!"

When their very own house appeared up ahead…

it was already late.
There were stars overhead!

So, without hesitation,

the two of them said:

“Twinkle, twinkle, little star,
how I wonder what you are.
Up above the world so high,

like a diamond in the sky.
Twinkle, twinkle, little star,
how I wonder what you are."

And Skinny Doug said:
"I love it, I love it!
Hip, hip, and hooray!
What a beautiful rhyme
for the end of the day.

Goodbye and good night, dear Bonnie and Ben.
We'll say some more rhymes when we all meet again."

And not long after that,
in their room down the hall,

young Bonnie and Ben said . . .

nothing at all!